蚂蚁和西瓜

[日]田村茂 文/图　蒲蒲兰 译

二十一世纪出版社

在一个好热的夏天的下午，

蚂蚁们发现了一块西瓜。

真好吃，赶紧搬回家吧。

快把大家喊过来吧。

哇！太棒了！

嗨——哟！

一、二，嗨——哟！

哎呀，怎么不动呀！

那么……

用铲子吧……

大家——搬呀搬！拼命——搬呀搬！

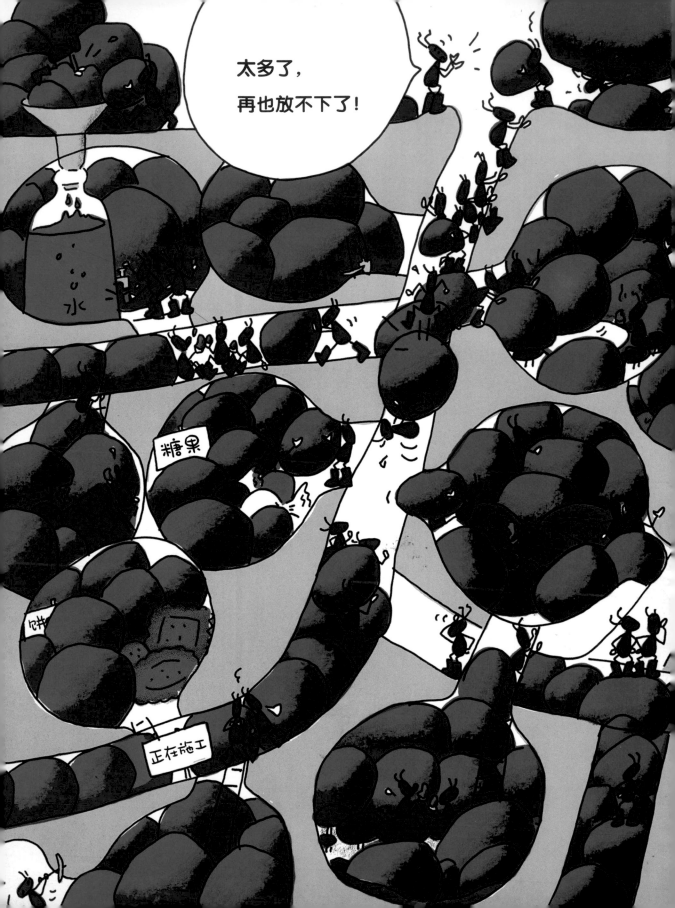

好！剩下的大家一起吃掉吧！

哎呀！吃得太饱了！

那么，把这个东西搬回去做……

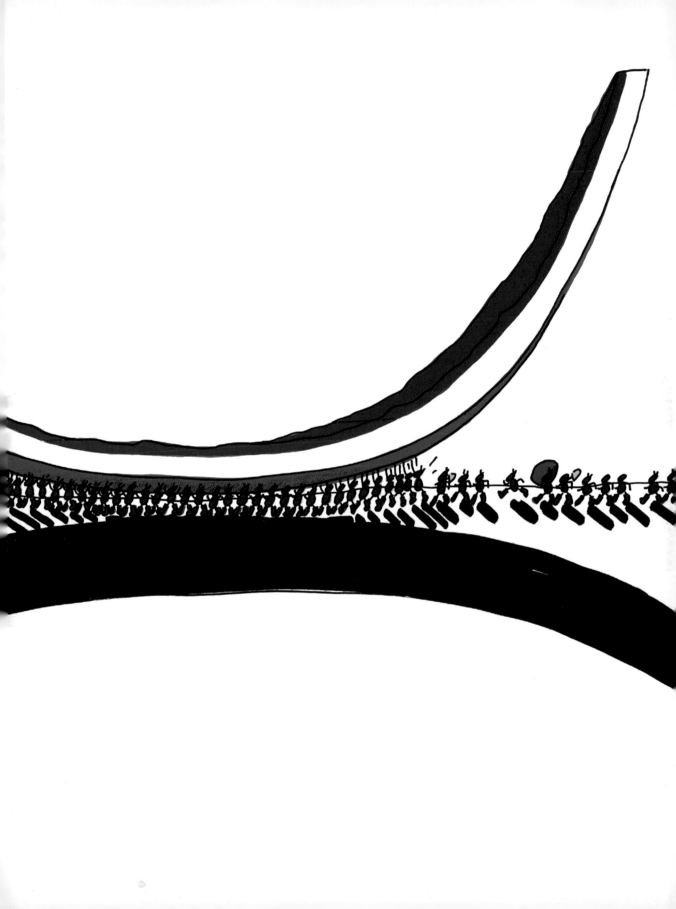

蚂蚁的西瓜滑梯！

一块西瓜在蚂蚁看来，多么的庞大，多么的诱人！

为了把好吃的西瓜带回家，蚂蚁们集体出动……先把家里装满，再疼快地饱餐一顿，最后还在西瓜皮上玩滑梯。

蚂蚁是一种可爱的小动物，也是在生活中处于弱势地位的孩子们的象征，蚂蚁和孩子之间总有着某些相似之处。一群小蚂蚁、一块大西瓜，对比强烈，故事简单而有趣，这也是作者精心的构思所在。孩子们一定会沉浸在这种简单的快乐中，同时，也会被蚂蚁们的勤劳、乐天、聪明和团结合作的精神而感染。

田村茂（TAMURA，Shigeru）

1949 年生于日本东京，毕业于桑泽设计研究所。他以富于诗意和幽默的作风独树一帜，在绘本、漫画、影视等领域发表作品，广受欢迎。本书是他的处女作，小东西遇到大的存在……是奠定他作品基调的风格之作。

The Deep Blue Sea

Bijou Le Tord

A PICTURE YEARLING BOOK

Published by
Bantam Doubleday Dell Books for Young Readers
a division of
Bantam Doubleday Dell Publishing Group, Inc.
1540 Broadway
New York, New York 10036

ISBN: 0-440-41063-0

Reprinted by arrangement with the author

Printed in the United States of America

March 1996

10 9 8 7 6 5 4 3 2 1

DAN

To my editor
Karen M. Klockner

"His strength was the flowers,
his dance was the clouds."
Miguel Angel Asturias

God
made the
earth.

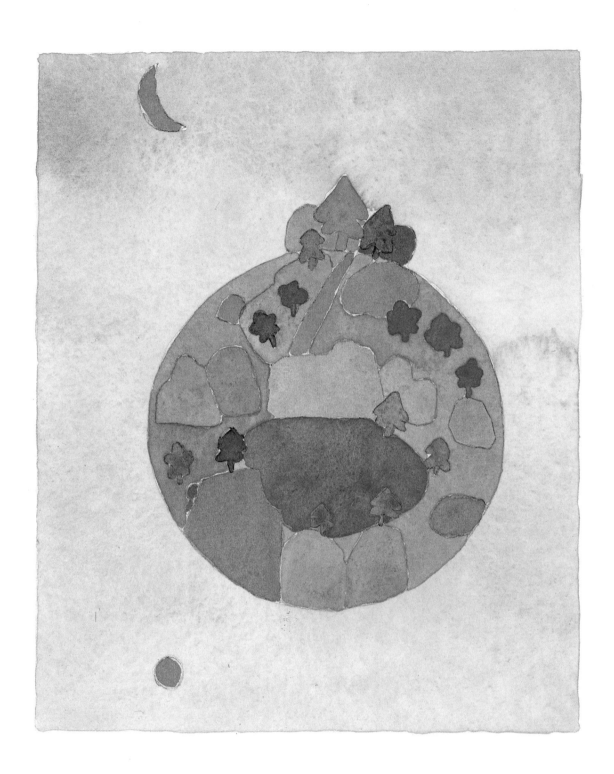

The sun
to warm
the days.

The moon
to cool
the nights.

And
the stars
to twinkle,
quietly.

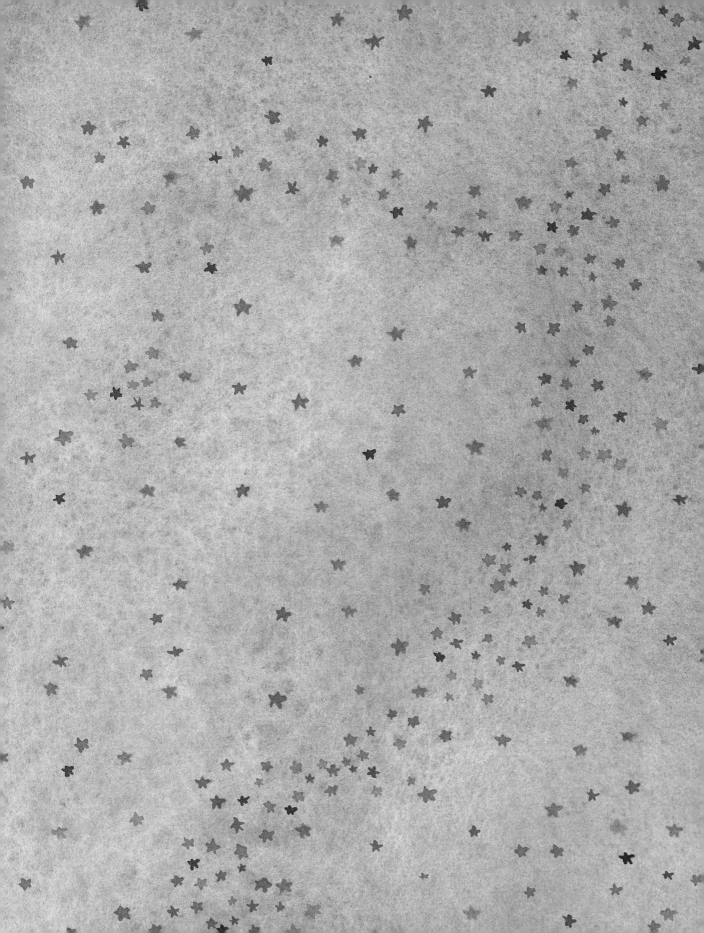

He let
drops of
rain fall
for seeds
to grow.
He planted
trees
with roots
deep in
the ground.

He planted
corn
for its yellow
grain.

He let
the streams
and rivers
flow
for birds
to nest in
cattails,
for ducks
to swim
in ponds,
and for
little frogs
to hop
on lily pads.

He made
mountains
for eternity.
Coyotes
for the desert,
snakes for
dust and
sand.

Prairie dogs
and buffaloes
for the open
plains.

He made
the wind,
the clouds,
and the deep
blue sea
for whales
to live harmoniously,

and sing
to their
sleeping
calves.

For the black-tailed gull
to swoop in
the swell of
the waves,

for the sandpiper
to feed on
tiny shrimp
and snails.

God
made volcanos,
tigers and
flowers,
bees with
honey.

He made
man and woman
to love
each other

and their children
and
their families.

He gave them
the earth
and the
planets.

He saw
that it was
all good.

God
made the
earth,
the sun,
the moon,
and the
stars
to twinkle
quietly,

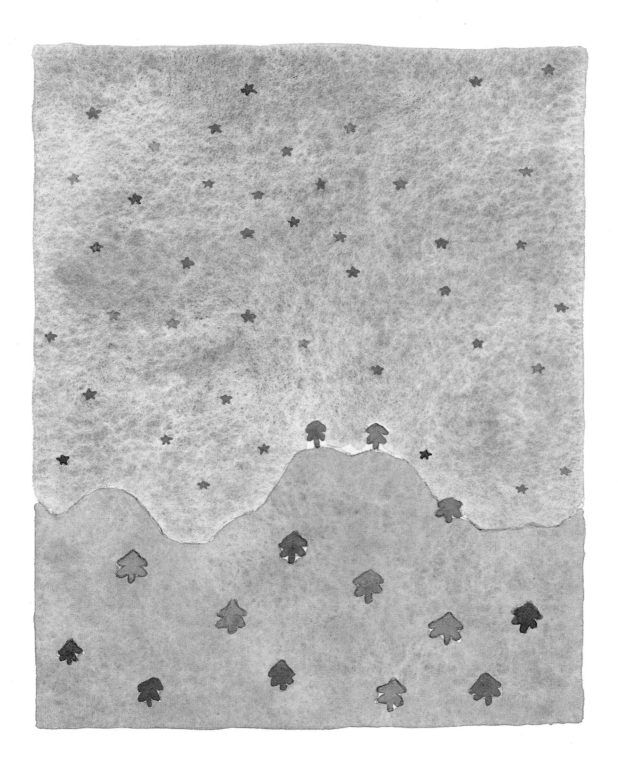

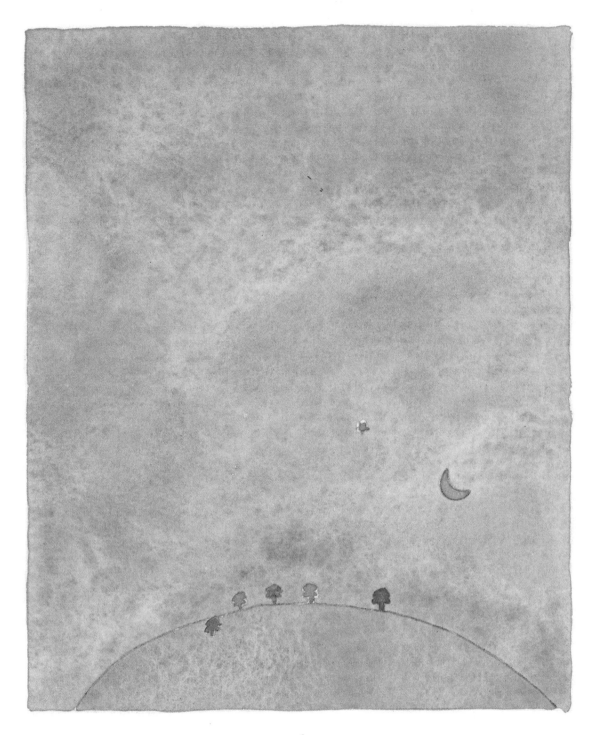

and
forever.